Blood Orange
Sky

James White

ISBN 978-1-64670-195-7 (Paperback)
ISBN 978-1-64670-196-4 (Digital)

Covenant Books
11661 Hwy 707
Murrells Inlet, SC 29576
www.covenantbooks.com

Chapter 1

The desert can bring illusions to one's eyes when he or she has been out there too long.

Frank had been traveling now for four days and three nights and had just ran out of water a few hours before. He was tired, hungry, and could drink a well dry right now. The only thing in sight was the hot southwest sun and blinding sand. He crossed a ridge and couldn't believe his eyes—there, in a beautiful valley just on the edge of the desert sand, was a house. He shook his head to gather his senses and hoped he wasn't hallucinating. He gently got on his horse, which was every bit as tired and thirsty as Frank, and rode toward the house, slow and easy. Frank had been around long enough to know one just doesn't go riding up on someone's property without them knowing who's coming.

He yelled loudly, "Hello, is anyone home? I come in peace. I just need water for me and my horse."

Frank saw the barrel of a rifle pointing out of the front porch window and heard a voice say, "Go on. I don't have anything for you. Best you went on your way." It was the voice of a woman, but Frank still hesitated; in these parts, it didn't matter if a person was a man or woman, for that person would be likely to get shot by either at the wrong place at the wrong time.

"I don't mean any harm. I just need water for me and my horse," Frank calmly said again. He slowly took off his holster and guns and laid them on the ground. "Please, I'll be willing to pay for water and food if you can spare any."

The rifle disappeared from the window, and the front door slowly opened. The woman looked at Frank and said, "Get off your horse and step away from your guns and take off your hat."

Frank slowly got down and stepped aside.

The woman came out of the house and asked, "What the hell are you doin' way out here? Trying to get yourself killed?"

"I'm just passing through, ma'am. Heading up to Santa Fe," Frank replied.

"What kind of business you got in Santa Fe?" the woman asked.

"I'll be glad to explain over a meal and a glass of water, ma'am, if you can spare any," Frank said desperately.

"Well's over there. Cups hangin' on the pump. Help yourself. You can put your horse in that old barn. There's a bucket in there to fill with water and some hay too," the woman said.

"'Preciate it, ma'am." Frank said.

She waited on the porch while Frank tended to his horse. When he finished, she invited him into the house and fixed him a plate of food. "Now then. Santa Fe, was it? What kind of business do you have there?" she asked.

Frank noticed her voice was kinder and more gentle now, thinking maybe she might trust him. "Well, ma'am, I work for the marshal there," Frank replied.

"What kind of work do you do for the marshal?" she asked.

"I'm a bounty hunter, more or less. I chase after criminals who escape and run from the law," Frank replied. "That's what brings me through here. I'm coming back from Old Mexico, where I was chasing a runaway."

"Did you find him?" she asked.

"Yes. Turned out he wasn't wanted in Mexico. I found him hangin' from a tree with a note pinned on his chest that said, 'Americans, stay out if you're running from the law.'" Frank said with a halfcocked grin.

She handed him a plate of food and said, "Sorry, this is all I have. It's vegetable beef soup with bread."

"This will do just fine, ma'am. Thank you very much," Frank said kindly.

"You can quit calling me ma'am. It makes me sound old. I'm only twenty-eight for God's sake. And my name is Rebecca, but I like to be called Becca," she said boldly.

4

"What are you doin' out here alone, ma'am—I mean, Becca—if you don't mind me asking?" Frank asked.

"I wasn't alone until a month ago. My husband got sick and was bedridden for a while and died," Becca said, wiping away tears. "I think he was bitten by a spider or something. I kept thinking he was gonna come out of it, but one night, he stopped breathing and died. I buried him out back in a little grove. We had been together for ten years. He was my first love and a damn good man."

The sound of horses came riding up outside, and a voice shouted, "You all right, Becca? We came to see if you might be needing things."

"Who is that?" Frank asked.

"Shh, don't let them hear you. I'll take care of this. Don't let them know you're here," Becca said quietly. She walked out to the porch and was talking to one of them for a minute. They left some things on the porch and went back the way they came from. Becca returned and had a very uneasy look on her face.

Frank knew something wasn't right about those men. "Who were those men?" Frank asked while he rolled a smoke.

Becca was very quiet now, and Frank couldn't help but ask again who those men were. She sighed and slowly explained, "The man I was talking to is young William O'Leary, the son of the wealthiest man in this county and probably the next one too. He's made a fortune from cattle and land that he basically stole from people and then drove them away from their ranches to steal them. He also owns the feed store in town, and it's the only one around for miles."

"I get the picture," Frank said sharply. "Young William is a spoiled little brat who is protected by his father."

"And it's best that they don't know you're here. That would bring trouble for me and you," Becca said.

"Why would them knowing I was here bring trouble for you, Becca?" Frank asked.

"Well, for a while now, Mr. O'Leary has been after us to have us sell this ranch to him, and he has offered a good price. But my husband plainly told him it isn't for sale. Since then, it's been hard for us to get credit anywhere in town, and it has taken a toll on us. And with my husband gone, I honestly don't think I'll be able to keep it," she said with disappointment.

"Do you have any family or anyplace else to go?" Frank asked.

"My brother lives in Missouri with his wife and three kids, but I wouldn't want to burden them with my circumstances. They have a small farm just north of Kansas City. It's a beautiful place," she explained. "I don't know what I'm gonna do, Frank. It's late, and I'm turning in. You're welcome to sleep in the bunk out in the barn. It's nothing fancy, but it's clean. You'd best be on your way in the morning."

Chapter 2

Frank had been asleep for a couple of hours when he was awakened by the sound of cattle running in the distance. He got up and went outside and walked a little way toward the sound of the cattle. He came to a ridge and saw forty or fifty heads of cattle and a half a dozen men with them. One man was yelling and Frank recognized the voice as young William O'Leary. He returned to the barn and was met by Becca standing at the door.

"Well, I guess you see now how O'Leary makes his money," Becca said.

"Yeah, looks like they're headed south to Mexico in a hurry. I'm guessing that herd of cattle doesn't belong to them," Frank said. Frank couldn't help but notice how beautiful Becca was, standing there in the moonlight with her long hair and thin figure.

"How old are you, Frank?" Becca asked. "You look like you've had a hard life, but don't look to be much in your thirties."

"I just turned thirty-five last month. And yes, I've had a harder life than I wanted, that's for sure," he said with that halfcocked grin of his.

"How long have you been doin' this kind of work?" she asked.

"About five years now, and it's starting to take its toll on me. I'm not much on riding long hours in the saddle anymore. You mind if I smoke, Becca?" Frank asked politely.

"No, I don't mind, Frank. My husband would have one now and then himself. I never touched them. Couldn't see the satisfaction in them, I guess," Becca said.

"You know, Becca, I don't have to be in Santa Fe for a while. I could stay here and help you fix up the place a little if you like," Frank replied.

"I don't know if that's a good idea, Frank. That could mean a lot of trouble for you if you stick around here," Becca replied.

"You let me worry about that trouble, Becca. You want the help or not?" Frank asked.

"Well, I could sure use the help, Frank. I guess I've let this place go since my husband died," she said.

"That settles it. We'll start with that broken fence around your corral first thing in the morning," Frank said.

"Okay then. That sounds great, Frank! I'll see you in the morning," Becca said.

"Good night, Becca. Sleep well," Frank replied.

*****

Frank woke to the smell of bacon coming from the house. He got up and walked outside to a majestic orange sky that he had either not paid much attention to or had now thought that there was just something magical about this place.

"Come on in, Frank. I have breakfast ready, then we can start on that old corral," Becca said through the kitchen window.

Frank took a deep breath and walked inside and said to Becca, "Sorry, I overslept a little. I haven't slept in a comfortable bed for a while."

"That's okay. Don't know how comfortable that old bunk is, but my breakfast is to die for. So my husband always said, that is," Becca said, smiling.

They sat and ate their breakfast, and Frank couldn't help again but notice how beautiful Becca was and tried to keep from staring at her. They finished eating, and Frank said, "Your husband was right. That was a to-die-for breakfast. Damn good. Thank you."

Becca smiled and blushed a little and said, "Glad you liked it, Frank."

They went out to start on the corral. It wasn't too bad; it just needed some straightening and some repairs.

*****

It was almost noon when they finished and heard the sound of horses riding up unexpectedly. It was Mr. O'Leary and a couple of his hired hands.

"Good afternoon, Becca, and what a fine afternoon it is. I see you fixed that corral. I hope this means you have considered my offer, and it is a mighty good offer," O'Leary said with an Irish accent. He glared at Frank. "Who might this fella be?"

Becca hesitated and then said, "This is my brother from Missouri. He's come to help me get on my feet."

"Ah. Brother, is it? Come to take your sister back to Missouri have ya, laddy?" O'Leary asked sharply.

"My sister does as she pleases, sir. My name is Frank. Who might you be?" Frank asked.

"William O'Leary, but most people around here call me Mr. O'Leary," he shouted.

"Sounds like you're an important man," Frank said with sarcasm.

"Tell me, Frank, what part of Missouri do you come from?" O'Leary asked.

Frank remembered the conversation he and Becca had about her brother who lives in North Missouri. "A little place just north of Kansas City," Frank said but was immediately interrupted by Becca.

"I'll consider your offer, Mr. O'Leary. Just give me a week to think it over, and I'll give you my answer then."

"A week it is, Becca. You and your brother take care of the place, and I'll see you in a week." O'Leary shouted as he rode away.

Frank looked at Becca and said, "Brother?"

"Well, it was the only thing I could think of unexpectedly, Frank," Becca said. "Those are some bad men, and I don't want any trouble."

"You keep saying trouble. Why are you so afraid of them?" he asked.

"They don't take no for an answer, that's why, Frank," she said.

"Yeah, I kind of got that feeling about him," Frank replied as he watched them ride away. "Well, we better get started on this barn don't you think, Becca?"

"Yes, I think so," she replied.

"We're probably gonna have to go in town tomorrow to get some lumber and nails and whatever else we need," Frank said.

Becca looked at him with a puzzled look and said, "I don't have any credit anywhere in town and no money to buy anything, Frank."

Frank looked at her calmly and said, "You let me worry about that. We'll get what we need, and I promise you that, pretty lady."

Chapter 3

The next morning, Frank woke up a little earlier and went outside to walk around and have a smoke. He thought to himself that he should go down to the only stream of water around for miles to wash up a bit. To his surprise, he saw Becca standing in it, naked, washing her soft bronze body. Frank had never seen anyone as beautiful as Becca, and he thought to himself on why he hadn't settled down with someone somewhere and raised kids by then. He thought, *Hell, I'm too old for that now. Who would want me?*

Becca looked up and saw Frank standing there. To his surprise, she smiled and said, "I'll be finished in a minute, Frank, and then it's all yours. The water is so refreshing this time of morning. You should bathe yourself."

Frank felt a little embarrassed and uneasy and said with a crack, "Yes, ma'am, I think I should."

Becca stood straight up and walked toward Frank and then right past him and said, "I'll have breakfast ready in half an hour. Come on in when you're done, Frank."

Frank was stunned by her beauty and found himself short of breath and couldn't say a word. He finished his bath and went to the house and sat down at the table to a hot cup of coffee and a plate of food fit for a king. He was still a little uneasy and didn't know what to say.

Becca asked, "How was the water, Frank? Refreshing?" She giggled a little.

"Fine, just fine," he said nervously.

"I have a wagon out back if you wanna hook it up to the horses, and we'll go into town and see if we can't get ourselves killed," she said with a laugh.

Frank laughed back and said, "That sounds just fine, Becca. Do you know if there's a telegraph office in town?"

"Yes, right next to the feed store, Frank," Becca answered.

Frank hooked up the wagon and brought it around to the front of the house, and Becca was standing there in a dress that just absolutely left him speechless again. Becca said to him, "Well, don't just stand there and stare, Frank. Help me in the wagon."

Frank tried to keep it together and helped her into the wagon, and they were on their way. They reached town in little over an hour. Frank was looking around and saw people walking about; there were probably a dozen merchants, a barber shop, a hotel with a saloon, and a café. *Typical town anywhere*, Frank thought to himself. Frank pulled the wagon in front of the general store and said to Becca, "I'll be right back."

He went to the telegraph office, which was right next door, and wired the marshal in Santa Fe. He walked outside and saw young William O'Leary and a couple of men standing by the wagon talking to Becca. Frank could tell that Becca was not comfortable. "What's the problem here, fellas?" Frank asked boldly.

"Just having a word with your sister," young William said.

"Well, it doesn't look like she wants to have a word with you." Franks voice was like a sharp knife as he spoke.

"Well, seems we have ourselves a live one here, boys," young William shouted as the other two men walked toward Frank.

"Boys, it would be in your best interest to turn around and walk away," Frank said sharply.

One of the men had a club in his hand and took a swing at Frank. Frank grabbed the club and took it away from the man and hit the other man with it and knocked him out cold. The other man came at Frank; Frank punched him, and he hit the ground like a sack of bricks. He turned and looked at young William and said, "Do you wanna end up like them, or are you smarter than they were?"

"I don't know who you are, mister, but you just bought yourself a whole lot of trouble," Young William said as he walked away.

"That seems to be a popular word around here," Frank shouted back at him. "Are you all right, Becca?"

"Yes, I'm okay, Frank. Let's just get what we need and get the hell outta here before young William returns with more men," Becca said.

They went inside the general store, and the owner told them he couldn't sell them anything by orders of Mr. O'Leary. Frank pulled out his US Marshal badge and told the man to give him what he needs by order of the US Marshal in Santa Fe.

The owner said to Frank, "Yes, sir. I'm sorry, sir. We've learned to do as we're told to do around here by O'Leary and his band of thieves."

"I don't answer to O'Leary, and you shouldn't either," Frank said as he shook the man's hand.

They got what they needed and loaded up the wagon and started back toward Becca's ranch. Becca was quiet as they were riding back, and Frank asked her, "Are you upset with me, Becca?"

"No, I'm not upset with you, Frank. But I am worried about what might happen to us now that you kicked the shit out of a couple of O'Leary's men."

"Don't you worry your pretty little self, Becca. I've been dealing with men like O'Leary my whole life, and I'm losing my patience with them," Frank said to her with a red face.

"Did you have to beat the shit outta them, Frank?" Becca asked.

"I guess I didn't like the way they were making you uncomfortable, and I lost my temper," Frank said.

Becca smiled a little and said, "Well, I guess they deserved it."

Frank smiled back with that crooked grin and felt really good for the first time in a long time.

*****

They arrived at the ranch about an hour before dark. While Frank was tending to the horses, Becca was inside, cooking supper. Frank could smell how good it was gonna taste. He thought to himself, *Am I here in this little piece of heaven with this beautiful woman? Or is this just an illusion? Maybe I'm really face-down in the desert somewhere, dying of dehydration, dreaming about all of this.* Just then, he heard Becca scream, and he ran to the house to find her standing on a chair in the kitchen, looking down at a scorpion on the floor. Frank stepped on it and threw it outside.

"That must have been what got your husband. Those little fellas carry a lot of poison and can be fatal if you're allergic. Your husband must have been allergic, Becca. I'm sorry," Frank said kindly to Becca.

Becca jumped off the chair and wrapped her arms around Frank so tight he could hardly breathe, and she wept like a little girl. She carried on about how much she loved her husband and thought they would always be together and how alone she's been since his death. Frank just held her and let her get all of that out; she obviously was needing to do just that. Frank was wondering if he could comfort her more, but holding her seemed to be working just fine.

Becca stepped back and wiped away her tears and said, "I'm sorry, Frank. I'm an emotional wreck, and I don't know what to do."

Frank took his right thumb and wiped away a tear in her eye and said, "Don't you worry, beautiful. Everything is going to be all right. I promise you that. Now come on, let's eat this to-die-for supper that smells so damn good."

She laughed and smiled and said, "Okay, Frank, I believe you."

They finished supper and moved out to the front porch, and Frank began to roll a smoke when Becca asked, "Why aren't you married, Frank? You're a good-looking guy who could have just about anyone you wanted. What's your story?"

Frank smiled and said, "Oh, it's probably my line of work. I'm not in the same place too long and never really considered it, I guess."

"Did you ever have a woman in your life, Frank?" Becca asked.

"A long time ago. We were very young. Her name was Molly, and she was so full of life and so pretty," Frank said softly.

"What happened, Frank?" Becca asked curiously.

"I went to see her one afternoon at her parent's ranch, and when I was riding up, I knew something wasn't right. I went inside and found Molly and her family shot to death," Frank said with emotion.

"Oh my God, who would do that, Frank?" Becca asked.

"Nobody could prove who did it, but I knew. It's the same story that's happening right here in this town. A tyrant son of a bitch trying to take over the land and wouldn't take no for an answer. The judge awarded their ranch to this Sullivan guy a week later. I knew what happened, and I knew I couldn't do anything about it at the time. So I rode outta there and kept riding as far as I could," Frank said.

"Then what did you do, Frank?" Becca asked.

"A month later, I joined with my brother and a few friends and decided we were gonna put a stop to Sullivan and his men, and we began robbing the places he owned and stealing back the horses and cattle he stole from others and gave the money and the animals back to the people he took it from. Word spread quickly of this modern-day Robin Hood and his band of brothers. But soon, it would turn against us, and we were wanted by the law. We went on with that for a while until my brother was shot and killed, along with a few others. And some were captured." Frank said as he rolled another smoke.

"What about you, Frank? What happened to you?" Becca asked.

"I left, moved out to California, changed my last name, and studied law. Ten years later, I came to New Mexico and turned myself in to the marshal in Santa Fe. He took me to the governor's office, and he gave me full amnesty. The marshal asked me to become his deputy, and that's where I've been since," Frank replied.

"What did your last name used to be, Frank?" Becca asked.

"James, but now it's Wilson," he said.

"You're Frank James, the brother of Jesse James?" she asked.

"That's who I was, but now, I'm Frank Wilson," he said.

"Well, Frank Wilson, I'm going to bed. We have a barn to fix tomorrow. Good night," she said with a smile.

"Good night Becca. Sleep well," Frank replied.

Chapter 4

Frank woke in the morning to the sound of raindrops rhythmically playing its tune on the roof of the old barn. It didn't rain much in this part of the world, so it was extremely well-appreciated when it did rain. Frank knew the O'Learys were coming. He just wasn't sure when they would come, but he figured soon. He gathered his senses—what was left of them anyway—and walked toward the house. Becca saw him and yelled for him to come in the house. Frank could smell her cooking, and his mouth began to salivate like the Niagara Falls. As he stepped inside, he took one look at Becca, and his tongue hit the floor. *She is a beauty from beyond this world,* he thought to himself.

"Good morning, Frank," Becca said cheerfully.

"And what a wonderful morning it is, Becca," Frank said. "I love the smell of fresh rain."

"It sure does brighten things up after it clears, doesn't it, Frank?" Becca replied. "You still wanna work on that old barn this morning?"

"Sure. This rain won't bother me at all. How 'bout you, Becca? You still interested?" Frank asked while he took a sip of coffee.

"Sounds good to me, Frank," she responded.

He noticed something different about her today. Her hair was slightly curled, and she smelled prettier than a garden full of spring flowers. Again, he found himself thinking—here he was, in the middle of nowhere, with the most beautiful woman he had ever seen in his life and was not too sure what to do about it. He looked at Becca and said, "You sure are a pretty lady. What would you say if I asked you to take a ride with me later when the rain stops?"

"Hmm, I think I'd say yes, Frank. I feel comfortable going anywhere with you," she said with a flirting smile and blushing cheeks.

Frank grinned with one side of his mouth, as he always does, and said, "Great! Let's get started on that barn, and maybe the rain will let up by noon."

Most of what they repaired was on the inside of the barn, so they were kept dry while it rained. It was going on noon when it let up and the clouds broke free and the sun came out and everything was a beautiful shade of blue and orange. It was a gorgeous sight to behold.

"How 'bout that ride now, Frank? This stuff can wait," Becca asked.

"Okay, I'll get the horses ready," Frank said with delight.

"I'll pack some food to take with us," Becca said.

They were shortly into their ride when Frank asked, "So how did you and your husband meet if you don't mind me asking?"

"I don't mind, Frank," she replied. "Well, my family and I lived in Oklahoma. That's where I was born and raised. My father had a general store in Oklahoma City, and I was working the register that day when in walked a couple of soldiers from the army. One of them kept staring at me and came up to say hi. Long story short, he was stationed outside the city, and we started seeing each other and fell in love. He was twenty-two, and I was eighteen. He only had a few months left in the army. He asked me to marry him, and we moved out here. This ranch was his family's ranch. His mother and father passed, so it was his now. We were doing great until he got sick and..." She started to cry and couldn't finish her story.

"I'm sorry, Becca. It sounds like he was a good man. What happened to your parents?" he asked.

"My mother died of influenza six years ago, and my father died a year later, probably of a broken heart. He loved my mother more than the world," she said as she wiped away tears. "My brother sold the store and moved to Kansas City with his wife and children."

"Why is it you don't have kids, Becca? I'm sorry, I shouldn't have asked you that," Frank said apologetically.

"No, it's okay, Frank. I don't know why we didn't have kids. We tried but never could. I don't know if it was me or him. Maybe I wasn't meant to have children," Becca said with disappointment.

"Don't be ridiculous. You're young, and maybe you'll still get that chance," Frank said, trying to cheer her up.

"I hope so, Frank. I love kids and would love to have at least one," Becca said with desperation.

They came upon a beautiful little spot on the river where the rainwater was trickling down through it and was singing a pleasant song as it flowed. It was the perfect spot for a picnic. Frank unpacked the horses while Becca spread a blanket on the ground under a tree and set out the food she packed for them. Frank turned and looked at her, sitting on the blanket; the sunshine was glowing through her beautiful light-brown hair, and she was radiating with beauty. He walked over and sat next to her on the blanket and couldn't believe how nervous he was. He'd been in situations with outlaws and crazy men and couldn't remember being this nervous.

Becca smiled at him and asked, "Are you okay, Frank? You seem a bit nervous?"

"I've never felt better in my life, Becca. I feel like a young man again, sitting on this blanket with you," Frank said happily.

"You're not old, Frank," she laughed.

"Can I ask you something, Becca?" Frank asked.

"You can ask me anything, Frank," she replied.

"Well, I guess I just need to come out and say it. I think you are the most beautiful woman I have ever seen, and I have this feeling in my stomach about you. And, if you don't mind, I'd like to stay here with you if that would be all right?" he said anxiously. "I've never met anyone like you and I can't stop staring at your beautiful face."

She looked at him with tears in her eyes and said, "I have that same feeling in my stomach, Frank. I've had it since you got here. I don't understand it, but maybe it was meant to be for us to find each other," she said as she stared into his eyes. "What about your job with the marshal?"

"I think it's time I quit that line of work. I'm not too fond of being in a saddle twelve hours a day anymore. I have money saved, and we could make a life here on your ranch if you want to stay," he said.

"I would love to stay, Frank, but what about O'Leary? What will we do about him?" she asked.

"I'll take care of them. Don't you worry. Those men will not be a problem much longer," he said sharply.

"I trust you, Frank, but it won't be easy with O'Leary. He won't give up easily," Becca said.

"I know, I know. I don't want you worrying about O'Leary," Frank said as he put his hand on her face and brushed her hair back and kissed her with more passion than he has ever felt in his life. He then said to her, "Everything is going to be okay."

Frank noticed the horses were restless and looked behind them and could see smoke in the distance. He knew it was Becca's place. "Come on, we need to get back. Can you ride fast?" he asked.

"Like the wind, Frank. Let's go," she said.

They made it back to the ranch, but the barn was almost gone. Nobody was there, but they knew who did this. "Look, there's a note on the door!" Becca screamed.

Frank grabbed it and read it aloud, "This is your first warning. Next time, it will be your house. Leave now, and go in peace." Frank crumbled the note in his hand and had a glare in his eyes that kind of scared Becca.

"What are you going to do, Frank?" she asked.

"It's time to let this O'Leary know that we are not leaving and he is not taking this ranch," he said sharply. "I have to go into town tomorrow and have a talk with O'Leary."

"I'm going with you, Frank. I'm not staying here alone," she said.

"All right. We'll be all right. They won't be back out here tonight," Frank said.

"I want you to sleep with me tonight, Frank, okay?" Becca asked.

"I would love that, Becca. Are you sure that's what you want?" he asked.

"Yes, it's okay. I know my husband would have wanted me to move on, and I'm sure he would approve of you, Frank," she said with a smile.

"We'll see to it that his ranch will thrive again, I promise you that, pretty lady," Frank said with a look on his face that made Becca somehow know that it would.

They watched as the barn disintegrated, and Frank told Becca not to worry because they will rebuild the barn. Becca took Frank by the hand and said, "I'm glad you came out of nowhere and rode up to my door, Frank. I don't know what would be happening right now if you weren't here."

"Yeah, I'm a believer in fate, Becca. And I believe mine is to be here with you," he said with a crooked smile.

"Let's go inside. I'll fix us supper, and then we can go to bed," Becca said.

"That sounds good to me, Becca," he replied as he smiled at her.

Chapter 5

Frank woke when the sun came shining through the bedroom window. Becca had her head on his chest, still asleep. He knew what he had to do today and somehow felt that it was all going to work out fine. He couldn't remember ever being happier than he felt right now. Once again, he asked himself if this was an illusion and if he was lying face-down in the desert somewhere, dying of dehydration. He sure hoped it was real; there was nowhere else he'd rather be than right here, right now, with this beautiful woman in this magical place.

Becca woke up and looked at Frank with her beautiful green eyes and said, "Good morning, Frank. Did you sleep well?"

"Better than I've ever slept in my life," Frank replied, smiling back as he kissed her on the forehead.

"Come on, Frank, I'll make us one of my to-die-for breakfasts before we go into town and get ourselves killed," Becca laughed.

"Well, if I'm gonna die, I'd much rather die with a full stomach," Frank laughed back.

*****

While they were at the table eating, a man came riding up to the house. Frank grabbed his rifle and went to the door and yelled, "Who the hell are you, and what do you want?"

The man yelled back and said, "I'm a messenger from the telegraph office. I have a message for Frank Wilson. It says it's urgent."

Frank could tell he was who he said he was and asked him to come down off his horse and have a cup of coffee before he rides back to town.

"Thank you, sir. I didn't get a cup this morning before I left. I sure would appreciate it," the man said kindly as he handed Frank the message.

Becca poured him a cup and gave him a couple slices of bacon she had left. "What is it, Frank?" Becca asked.

"A wire from the marshal in Santa Fe. Says he can be there in two days with an army outfit," Frank replied.

"So that's who you wired. I wondered about that," Becca said.

"Yeah. I figured we could use all the help we can get. I don't know if we can wait two days, though. O'Leary might send his men out here today if we don't get to him first," Frank said.

"O'Leary's gone, sir. He rode outta town last night. Pretty sure he was headed down to Mexico. Young William is in town with a dozen men or so. They've been in the saloon all night," the man said.

"Well, this might be the opportunity we need. Do you know where Becca can go and be safe while I deal with young William?" Frank asked the man.

"Sure. She can stay with my wife. We have a house on the west side of town. It should be easy getting her there without being seen," the man replied.

"Are you sure you're okay with that?" Frank asked the man.

"Mister, if there's a way to get rid of O'Leary and his band of thieves, then I'm in," the man said to Frank.

"What's your name, friend?" Frank asked.

"Tom, sir," he replied.

"Well, Tom, that is exactly what we are gonna do," Frank said.

"Frank, you're not going in there to talk to young William alone, are you?" Becca asked.

"I'll be fine, Becca. Don't you worry your pretty little self. Let's get our things and ride in with Tom," Frank said.

*****

They rode into town unseen. Tom took Becca to his house while Frank came in from another direction and rode to the feed store, where he was met by a couple of O'Leary's men. He got down from his horse, and the two men came walking toward Frank. One of them said, "You don't have any business here, mister. You're in the wrong place."

Frank opened his coat to one side and showed them his US Marshal badge and said, "I'm making it my business. Where is young William?"

"That badge doesn't mean a damn thing around here, mister," one of the men shouted.

"Well, the last time I checked, New Mexico is part of the United States, and this badge says US Marshal. So that makes me the law around here since there is no sheriff," Frank boldly said back to him.

One of the men drew his gun, but Frank was faster and shot him dead right there. The other man threw his arms up and said, trembling, "I don't wanna die today. Young William's in the saloon. Please, don't shoot, mister."

"Get on your horse, and ride outta here. And I better not ever see your face in this town again. Is that clear?" Frank shouted at the man.

The man got on his horse and bolted out of town like the wind. Frank went to the saloon and slowly walked inside, but there wasn't anyone there, except the bartender. Frank asked the bartender where young William, was and he pointed toward the back door. Frank went slowly to the door and opened it. There was a table and some chairs, and the room was still filled with smoke from the stench of nasty cigars. He saw another door that went outside and figured they probably heard the gunshot from Frank and took off.

Frank went back to the bartender and asked him where they went, and the bartender said, "Mister, it would probably be in your best interest if you left here and didn't come back, or you might get yourself killed."

Frank gave him a look of terror and said to him, "Do you wanna live in fear your whole life, or do you want peace and prosperity? I know you don't have either of those now, so tell me where I can find young William O'Leary."

Just then, a young girl came crawling out of the back room. She must have been hiding under the table, and Frank didn't see her. Her clothes were ripped to shreds, and she had bruises on her arms and face and didn't look to be fourteen or fifteen years old. Frank was boiling at this point; he knew what had happened to this young girl, and he helped her to sit in a chair. She was shaking and crying and said a few words in Spanish. Frank guessed young William brought her from Mexico. His Spanish wasn't good, but he could tell what she was saying.

"It's okay. You're safe now," Frank said to her as he took off his coat and wrapped it around her. "Now, where can I find these cowardly bunch of pigs?" he asked the bartender.

"Their ranch is five miles south of here. You'll know it when you see it. It's the biggest place around here," the bartender said.

*****

Frank took the girl to Tom's house, and Becca came running out to meet him and hugged him tightly and said, "I was so worried, Frank. We heard a gunshot. Are you okay?"

"I'm okay, Becca, but this girl needs some attention. Take her inside and clean her up and get her something to eat," Frank replied.

Tom's wife spoke Spanish and took the girl inside.

"What are you gonna do now, Frank?" Tom asked.

"The marshal is on his way but won't be here for a while, so I better head out to O'Leary's ranch and deal with young William and his men before O'Leary comes back with more men," Frank said furiously. "Young William needs to pay for what he's done here, and so does his father. And they better pray for their sake that I can stay on the right side of the law when I see them."

"Frank, you can't go alone. Wait till the marshal gets here with that army outfit," Becca pleaded.

"I can't wait, Becca. You stay here with Tom and his wife, and see to it that little girl gets help. I'll be back soon," he said.

"I'll go with you, Frank," Tom said.

"No, you stay here and look after the women. I have to go alone," Frank said.

"Frank, please be careful, and come back to me," Becca said as she wrapped her arms around him tightly.

"Don't you worry, beautiful. I'll be back as soon as I can. This has to be done now," Frank said to Becca as he kissed her on the forehead and then on her lips.

Chapter 6

Frank went to the general store to see if they had any rifles with ammo. The owner didn't hesitate; he gave Frank a brand-new rifle with plenty of ammo. "Good luck, mister," the general store owner said.

"This is gonna get ugly before it gets better," Frank said to the general store owner. "And I'll have to deal with Mr. O'Leary when he gets back from Mexico."

"I'll give you whatever you need, sir. My door is open to you," the store owner said.

"Thank you, kind friend. The marshal should be here tomorrow. If I'm not back by then, tell him where I went," Frank said.

"Yes, sir," the store owner replied.

Frank was six-feet-two-inches tall, and when he sat on a saddle, he looked even bigger. As he walked his horse through the town, he could feel every eye on him, knowing these people were counting on him. For some reason, Frank liked this town and the area surrounding it. He felt like he belonged here and had a sense of pride about him that he hadn't felt for a long time. He thought of Becca and how beautiful she was and how he got here in this chapter of his life. He had very much been alone since returning from California. He was educated and proud of how his life turned out since the days with Jesse and the gang. He thought of his childhood, growing up in Missouri—not far from where Becca's brother is living—and the trouble they used to get into when they were boys. He wondered how a boy who got into so much trouble found himself wearing a US Marshal's badge as a man. *Funny how life works out sometimes for people*, he thought.

He kept riding south and found a place to hold out until it got dark. He knew he couldn't just ride up and say hi; he had to wait for the cover of darkness if he had any chance at all. He tied his horse to a tree on a dry riverbed with high walls surrounding it. Frank figured this was a good spot to wait it out. He took out his .30-30, which the general store owner had given him, and filled it with ammo and did the same with his other guns. He figured young William, being the coward he was, would use his men as shields and put a few of them out front and at the back to surround him with protection. Frank had dealt with men like young William before. He wasn't too smart but had enough of Daddy's money to make him dangerous.

He sat there on a log sticking out of the side of the hill and rolled a smoke. He thought of Becca. He'd never met a woman like her, and she certainly melted his heart. He loved her soft bronze skin, tanned from the New Mexico sun for the last ten years. Once again, he found himself thinking if this was only a dream—was he lying face down in the desert, dying of dehydration and having an illusion, or was this real? *Yes, this is real,* he told himself. And he had better get it together, or he'd never see that beautiful woman again.

*****

It was turning dark and almost time to go. He packed his guns on his horse and climbed on and rode toward the O'Leary ranch. He stopped about half a mile before the house and tied his horse to a bush and started walking to the house. There wasn't a lot of cover—a few bushes and cactuses—but luckily, the moon wasn't full. He crept slowly until he was a hundred yards or so from the house. He could see the front porch and saw a light on the inside but didn't see anyone. He sat there a few minutes to see if anyone moved around. He heard horses riding away from the back of the house; it sounded like four or five horses. He walked toward the house slowly. He figured that could be a diversion.

He reached the fence and climbed over and went to the back of the house. He didn't hear or see anyone. He picked up a rock and threw it at a window, shattering it. Two men jumped out and started shooting wildly. Frank kicked the door open and dropped both men. One man was still breathing, lying on the floor, gasping for air. Frank stood over him and asked him, "Where the hell is Young William?"

The man could barely speak but uttered one word, "Town."

Frank's heart sank, and he turned pale. He knew they were probably going after Becca. He got back to his horse and jumped on frantically and rode like crazy back toward town, hoping he could reach Becca before they did.

He reached town. It was dark and quiet, and he knew something was wrong. He made his way to Tom and Elizabeth's home and quietly knocked on the door. Nobody answered. He turned the knob and went inside.

Tom was lying on the floor, badly beaten and bleeding but was alive.

"Where is Becca?" Frank asked.

Tom couldn't speak; he only shook his head. Frank knew young William had her and could only imagine the worst. Where would he take them, and how could he find her? Frank went for the doctor and told him about Tom.

A young boy came running up to Frank, breathing heavily, and said, "I know where they are going, mister. I saw them heading out of town."

"Which way did they go, boy?" Frank asked.

The boy pointed toward Mexico, and Frank said, "Of course, they're going to their place in Mexico. That's where O'Leary was hiding out."

Frank rode south in a bolt. There was only one way to cross the river that he knew of by horse and figured that it had to be where they were heading. He had to reach it before they got there, or he may never see Becca again. He hoped he could reach her before it was too late.

28

Chapter 7

It was well into the night when young William said it was time to rest the horses.

"Come on, this is a good spot to rest the horses. But we can't stay long. I'm sure Mr. Wilson is on his way," Young William said. Then he said with anger, "Donnie, you and your brother go up the hill and watch out for him. If you see him coming, don't shoot. Just ride down here quietly. You, women, get down off your horses, and sit down and shut up!"

He had a frightened and uneasy look about him, Becca noticed. He was pacing back and forth, talking to the other men. There were four of them, but she knew they were no match for Frank. She heard them talking but couldn't make out what they were saying. Something about Mexico, she heard.

"Dear God, they're taking us to Mexico," she said to Elizabeth.

"Why would they take us to Mexico?" Elizabeth asked.

"I don't know, but I hope Frank catches up to us before we get there," Becca responded.

"Mexico?" The young girl asked. Elizabeth spoke to her in Spanish and asked her why they would be taking them to Mexico.

"O'Leary's ranch is there, just across the border a few miles," the young girl said. "I was working there with my mother and father when young William took me to the US a few days ago."

Becca had an idea and took off her wrap from around her waist and stood behind Elizabeth and tied it to a tree, hoping Frank would notice it when he came through.

Young William yelled for Donnie and his brother to come on. They were movin' on. The women got back on their horses, and

Becca hoped to God they wouldn't see her wrap on the tree branch. The men got on their horses, and they started across the river.

*****

Frank had been riding hard and knew he was only thirty minutes or so behind them, and he hoped that he would catch up to them soon. He came down the hill toward the river crossing and could see a scarf or wrap on a tree branch and knew it was Becca's. She was okay, he thought, and sighed with relief. He saw the horse tracks and followed them into the river.

*****

Becca and the rest of them were crossing to Mexico when young William looked back at her and smiled and said, "Won't be long now. We'll be at our ranch, and your Frank will be out of his jurisdiction."

Becca looked back at him and shouted, "You better hope you drown in this river. When Frank gets to you, you'll wish you were already dead!"

Young William shouted back, "When I get through with you, you'll wish you would have drowned in this river too!"

*****

Frank could see them but knew he couldn't just ride out into the water, or he'd be a sitting duck. He went down the river a few hundred yards and found a place where he thought he could make it across. He had to get off his horse and swim with it, but he didn't have a choice. The current was strong, but he was a good swimmer; he had learned to swim back in Missouri as a boy. It took him downstream a bit, but he reached the other side and got on his horse and rode toward Becca. They were about a half mile away when he saw them and knew he couldn't just ride up on them. He didn't want to get the women killed. He followed them quietly for a while, waiting for the right moment to make his move.

*****

Becca had a feeling Frank was close by. She asked Elizabeth to ask the young girl how far O'Leary's ranch was. The young girl spoke in Spanish and said, "About an hour."

Becca knew Frank would have to do something soon before they got to the ranch, so she yelled at young William, "We need to stop for a minute. This young girl isn't feeling well."

"You'll have plenty of time to rest when we get to the ranch. Shut up, and keep riding," Young William shouted.

"The young girl is thirsty. She needs water!" Becca shouted back.

"Give her your canteen, Donnie!" Young William said.

"I don't have any left, boss. I drank it back at the crossing," Donnie said.

Young William turned his horse around and told everyone to stop. He grabbed his canteen and handed it to Becca and said, "Here, I need you to be healthy, pretty lady. As for the young girl, I don't need her anymore." He pulled out his pistol and shot her in the head, killing her instantly.

Becca and Elizabeth screamed and jumped off their horses and ran to the young girl. "You didn't have to do that, you animal! I hope you rot in hell!" Becca screamed at Young William.

They heard a rifle shot, and young William fell to the ground, dead. Frank had shot him with the brand-new .30-30 the store owner had given to him. He fired again, hitting one of the other men, and the other two took off like jackrabbits. Frank rode up to Becca and asked if she was all right.

"Yes, I'm okay Frank. It sure is good to see you," she said with tears running down her face. "Young William shot that poor little girl and said he didn't need her anymore."

"We don't have to worry about him anymore, but you can bet those other two men are riding straight for O'Leary to tell him I just killed his son," Frank said. "Let's bury this girl, and get moving."

Frank dug a grave, and they found some rocks to put on top of it so they could recognize it later. Elizabeth said a few words in Spanish, and they left. Frank knew they didn't have to ride hard but knew they had to keep moving and reach town before O'Leary caught up to them. They crossed the river, and Becca asked, "What are you going to do about O'Leary?"

"Hopefully, the marshal will be here soon. I don't know how many men O'Leary has in Mexico, but I'm sure they'll be coming for me when they hear young William is dead," Frank said. "What did you know about that young girl, Elizabeth?"

"Not much," she said. Elizabeth added with empathy, "Her mother and father worked at O'Leary's. She was very distraught. Those men did a lot of bad things to her."

"I know. Young William got what he deserved, and I'm looking forward to bringing O'Leary to justice as well," Frank said.

"What if the marshal doesn't get here before O'Leary does, Frank? What will you do, then?" Becca asked with fear in her voice.

"He'll be here, Becca. He's a man of his word," Frank said as he held her tightly in his arms. "Everything will be just fine. I promise you that, beautiful."

"I hope Tom is okay," Elizabeth said.

"Tom will pull through. He's a strong man. He was beaten up some, but I bet he's waiting for you to walk through that doctor's door anytime, Elizabeth," Frank said.

"Thank you, Frank. You sure have a way of making people feel better," Elizabeth said.

"He sure does. I don't know what would be happening now if you hadn't of come riding up to my front porch. I'm so glad you're here, Frank," Becca said smiling.

"Me too, beautiful, me too," Frank said, smiling back at her.

Chapter 8

As they were riding, Frank remembered Becca leaving her wrap on a tree branch by the river and said, "We'll take a short rest when we get to Becca's tree. No need in pushing our horses too hard."

Becca smiled and looked at Frank with her beautiful green eyes. They reached the tree, and Frank tied the horses where there was a little bit of grass for them to eat. He took his canteen from his saddle and handed it to Becca. She guzzled a little bit of it and handed it to Elizabeth.

"Thank you, Frank. You're a very kind man," Elizabeth said.

"I have some dried beef and biscuits from the general store. You two must be starving," Frank said.

They sat there and ate for a bit, as did the horses. The sun was coming up, and the sky was blood orange. "What a beautiful sight," Frank said. "We better get moving, we'll be back in town in an hour or so."

As they were riding back to town, Frank couldn't keep his eyes off of Becca. She was the most beautiful woman he had ever seen, and he knew in his heart that she was the one he wanted to be with for the rest of his life and would do whatever it takes to make that happen. He knew O'Leary was coming but didn't know how many men he would bring with him. He hoped the marshal would show up soon with that army outfit from Santa Fe.

Becca looked at Frank and could tell he was thinking about O'Leary and said, "We'll be all right, Frank. Everything will work out."

"I know, beautiful. I feel in my heart that we will prevail over this tyrant O'Leary, and you and I are gonna live a long and happy life together," Frank said, smiling at Becca with that crooked grin.

"You two lovebirds get moving before O'Leary catches up to us. You'll have plenty of time for all that later. I need to get to town and find Tom," Elizabeth said.

Frank and Becca smiled at each other and picked up the pace a little.

*****

It was early when they rode into town. There wasn't a lot of people out and about yet. They rode straight to the doctor's office to see Tom and was met by the doctor at the door.

"Is Tom okay?" Elizabeth asked.

"He was beaten pretty badly, but he's doing fine. He's sleeping now," the doctor said.

"Can I see him?" Elizabeth asked.

"All right, but be easy with him. He's bruised up pretty bad," the doctor said.

Elizabeth went inside and saw Tom sleeping, and he immediately woke up when she walked in. They had that kind of love between them that they completed each other's sentences. Elizabeth was crying and said, "Oh, Tom, I was so worried about you. Are you all right?"

Tom swallowed hard, and a tear came out of his badly bruised right eye and softly said to her, "My sweet Elizabeth, I will never leave you. Are you all right? Those men didn't hurt you, did they?"

"I'm okay, Tom, thanks to Frank. He killed young William O'Leary and one of the others while the other two men rode away as fast as they could ride," Elizabeth answered.

"It's so good to see you, my sweet. I was worried, but I knew Frank would bring you back to me. I owe him a debt of gratitude," Tom said.

"Now, you rest, Tom. The marshal will be here with that army outfit, and everything will be just fine," Elizabeth said as she kissed him on the forehead.

He squeezed her hand and fell asleep.

*****

Frank and Becca were standing outside when the general store owner walked over and asked Frank, "How'd that new Winchester work out for ya, Mr. Wilson?"

"Perfect. Thank you very much, my friend," Frank responded.

"Anything you need, sir, it's yours," the store owner replied.

"We'll need a room and bath for these women. I could use a bath myself, but I better get ready in case O'Leary shows up before the marshal gets here," Frank said.

"I'll take them to the hotel and get them a room and bath," the store owner said.

"Thanks, friend," Frank said to the man.

"What are you gonna do, Frank?" Becca asked.

"Try to find as many men as I can to help me defend against O'Leary when he comes," Frank said.

"Most men here are farmers and merchants, Mr. Wilson. Not much fight in them, I'm afraid," the store owner said.

"Well, it's time for them to learn that some things are worth fighting for if they want their freedom," Frank said.

"You can count on me, Mr. Wilson. I know my way around a rifle somewhat," the store owner said. "Come on, ladies, let's get you a bath and some clean clothes."

*****

Frank walked to the saloon. He figured he could count on the bartender to help him gather some men. The bartender was just opening up the bar when Frank walked in, and he could smell the fresh coffee in the air. "Good morning to you," Frank said.

"Good morning back. Looks like you got those girls back safe and sound," the bartender said.

"All, except the young girl. Young William shot her dead right in front of the others. Wasn't long, though. He met his maker," Frank said.

"Guess that means O'Leary will be looking for revenge since you killed his one and only son," the bartender said.

"No doubt he's coming. I need your help. The marshal's coming, but I don't know for sure when he will be here," Frank said.

"I'm a bartender, not a gunslinger. I'm afraid I wouldn't be much help," the bartender said.

Frank looked at him very seriously and asked, "How many men do you figure O'Leary has with him in Mexico?"

The bartender responded, "He always has a dozen or so with him and probably has another dozen in Mexico, so you're looking at twenty men or so."

"I could use your help. You know every man in town and could help me sort out who would be helpful and who wouldn't be," Frank said.

"Not many here. Most of these men are merchants and farmers. I doubt many know how to use a gun, let alone kill someone," the bartender said.

"We'll just have to find out, I guess," Frank said. "Does that old bell still ring across the street?"

"Yeah, it still rings loudly," the bartender replied.

Frank walked over to the bell and pulled on the rope until people started walking toward him. He yelled loudly and said, "All men are to meet in the saloon in fifteen minutes by order of the US Marshal's office."

*****

Frank went to the hotel to Becca's room and knocked on the door. Becca opened it, and Frank took one look at her, standing there, freshly bathed. Her hair was still damp, and she was wearing a dress that left him speechless.

"Yes, Frank, what do you want?" Becca said in a flirtatious voice.

He cleared his throat and said, "My God, you are beautiful. I came to check on you to see if you were okay."

"I'm fine, Frank. That was a much-needed bath. Are you okay, Frank?" Becca asked.

"I'll feel better when this is over and we can get on with our lives," Frank said.

"Is that all you wanted to tell me, Frank?" Becca asked, flirting again with those big, green eyes.

"No, that wasn't all I wanted to say, Becca," Frank said.

"Well, what else, Frank? You can say anything to me," Becca said softly.

Frank hesitated and waited for his heart to stop pounding and said, "Well, I love you, Becca. I've loved you since our first conversation. I knew then that I wanted to be with you for the rest of my life, and nothing is gonna stop us from being together."

Becca had a warm feeling come over her, and her face got red and thought to herself, *This is crazy.* But she felt the same way. She looked at Frank and smiled and said, "I love you too, Frank." She threw her arms around him and kissed him passionately and said, "I was hoping to hear those words from you."

"You're gonna hear those words for a very long time, beautiful lady. I promise," Frank said. "I have to go to the saloon and meet with the men. You stay here until this is all over, and I'll come for you." He kissed her and held her tight for a few seconds and walked to the saloon.

Chapter 9

Frank walked into the saloon, and to his surprise, there were about a dozen men inside. Frank walked over to the bartender and stood next to him. He knew the bartender would know everyone and could help him relate to them. Frank was a towering figure and stood taller than the rest of the men, with a good posture and personality to go with it. The men knew Frank was a deputy marshal, but they didn't know who he really was, and Frank wanted to keep it that way.

It was quiet, and Frank cleared his throat and sternly said, "I guess you all know why we're here. O'Leary has dictated this town long enough, and it's time we dethrone him. I shot and killed his son, young William, and a couple of others."

The men mumbled a little to each other in delight. "Young William is dead, and I hope he rots in hell for what he's done around here," one of the men shouted. All of the men shouted loudly with pleasure.

"All right, all right." Frank tried to calm them down. He then said, "That's only a few of O'Leary's men. He has more with him in Mexico, and I'm gonna need your help."

"I thought the marshal was coming in from Santa Fe with an army outfit?" one of the men shouted.

"He is, but it might be late evening before he gets here. We can't take that chance. O'Leary may be here this afternoon, so we need to be ready in case he does," Frank said.

"What do you propose we do, Mr. Wilson?" the bartender asked.

"How many of you know how to handle a rifle?" Frank asked.

Three of the men raised their hands, and another one shouted, "I hunted squirrels back in Tennessee when I was a boy."

"All right. Do any of you have rifles or guns of any kind?" Frank asked.

The general store owner shouted out, "I've got that covered, Mr. Wilson. I have a dozen of those .30-30 Winchesters at the back of my store with plenty of ammo. O'Leary himself ordered them a few weeks ago. I just never got around to tell him they arrived." He then chuckled.

"You're a good man. Let's go over to the general store and get ourselves familiar with these rifles and figure out who can shoot one." Frank grinned out of one side of his mouth.

*****

As they made their way to the general store, Frank was eyeing the buildings to see where to place some of the men. They went inside and gathered around while Frank and the store owner went to the back to collect the rifles. They lifted the box full of rifles and carried it to the front where the men were standing. Frank took a look at these men and wondered if they would be up to this task. These were businessmen and shopkeepers, not killers like O'Leary's men. He knew this was an unfair advantage if it were to happen.

Frank stood in the middle of the men and said, "This isn't squirrel-hunting, men. These are men with guns, and they'll be shooting back at you. And if any of you don't think you can do this, you can step out now. Nobody will say anything."

The men shook their heads and mumbled to each other. The general store owner spoke up and said, "Men, we're all businessmen here, not fighting men. But it's time we stood up to this tyrant O'Leary if we want our stores and our town back."

The men shouted with loud hoorahs.

"These are the finest rifles on the market right now. They hold nine shells and lever action with open sights. Just load, aim, and fire," the store owner said. He was passing out rifles to the men while Frank was looking at the men and felt good about it. He was hoping the marshal would be here by now, but he couldn't take any chances. O'Leary is coming and could be here any moment.

"All right, men, let's put together a strategy for this encounter we're about to incur," Frank said. "They'll be riding in fast and probably head straight to the saloon. Two of you get on the roof across the saloon and two more across from them. We'll stay in two's since there are twelve of you. Pair up, and stay together. Watch out for each other, and stay alive."

Frank positioned the other men, and he and the bartender went to the saloon. He told the bartender to act normal. "Don't be nervous, and you'll be all right. I'll be in the back room, watching and listening," Frank said. He went to the back room, where he found the young girl, and it gave him a sick feeling in his stomach. He saw the door that led outside and figured some of O'Leary's men would come in through that door. He went outside and saw an old shed a few steps from the back door and went inside and waited.

As he sat there, he couldn't help but think of Becca and how his life had led to this day right here, right now. He rolled a smoke and thought to himself on what would become of their relationship. He really loved her ranch; it was such a beautiful place with breathtaking scenery. He thought of her husband and what a decent man he must have been and how sad it was that he died. Then again, where would he be if her husband was still alive? Would he have this run-in with O'Leary and be sitting here in this woodshed? He couldn't think like that. He has an opportunity to be happy and in love, and by God, nobody was going to come between that. He had money saved in a bank in Santa Fe and could help Becca get her ranch fixed up and going again, and they could have a prosperous and happy life together.

He smiled and put out his cigarette and waited.

Chapter 10

About an hour passed by when Frank heard the sound of horses riding up the street, and he could tell some of them split off in a different direction. He could see six riders coming down the main street, but he couldn't see O'Leary. They were a mixed group of Irish and Mexicans. As he suspected, they rode to the saloon. The Mexican men waited outside while the Irish guys went inside the saloon. Frank couldn't hear what they were saying, but he waited to make a move to see if the other men came around.

Just then, he saw them coming from the other side of the town, and they rode to the back of the saloon where Frank was hiding. There were four of them but still no O'Leary. One of them got down from his horse and went inside through the back door. Frank was worried about the bartender. He couldn't wait; he had to make a move, or it might be too late. He knew he could take these three men on their horses, and he hoped the other men would do their part with the men in front.

Frank grabbed his revolvers and lunged out from the shed and began shooting rapidly until all three men were on the ground. Not one of them got a shot off; Frank was quick and accurate. One man came running out of the back door, and Frank shot him. He heard shooting around the front, and it sounded like a war zone. Then, it suddenly stopped.

Frank went inside and saw the bartender lying on the floor. He was badly beaten, but he was all right. Frank walked outside and saw O'Leary's men lying dead on the ground. The other men were walking toward the saloon. Frank yelled for someone to get the doctor.

The men came inside the saloon, and Frank said proudly, "Well, it seems you men adjusted yourselves to those rifles rather quickly. Nice shooting."

"What about O'Leary? He's not here," the general store owner said.

Frank adjusted his hat a little and said, "I don't know. Probably in Mexico, hiding like the coward, he is. But he's lost a lot of men now."

"What are we gonna do now, Mr. Wilson?" one of the men asked.

"I think we should hold off and wait for the marshal to get here. O'Leary isn't gonna do anything else today, I think," Frank said.

Becca came running across the street from the hotel and threw her arms around Frank and said, "I'm so glad you're all right, Frank. Is it over? Is O'Leary dead?"

Frank was smelling Becca's hair while she was hugging him and said to her, "I'm afraid not. He's not among these men, but I'm sure we'll see him soon." Frank gathered his senses. "Come on, men, we have graves to dig."

They buried those men in the cemetery outside of town, and they found it was hard to come up with decent words to say. But Frank knew it was the right thing to do to say a few words.

*****

It was late afternoon when they finished with the burials when they heard the sound of horses riding from the north. It was the marshal, and he only had a few men with him. They rode up to the cemetery where Frank and the men were, and the marshal said, "Well, looks like some things never change. I guess you had some trouble already, Frank."

"Yeah, that seems to be the popular word around here, Marshal. Good to see you. I thought you were bringing some army men with you?" Frank asked.

"It seemed the army had more important things on their agenda. They said this was a state matter, not a federal one. Kind of contradictive, isn't it?" the marshal said with a grin on his face.

"Like you said, Marshal, some things never change," Frank said sarcastically.

The marshal tipped his hat back and asked Frank, "So tell me, what kind of trouble is going on around here? Or do I need to ask?"

"Same old story, Marshal. One man and his money thinking he owns and controls the whole county," Frank said.

"Yeah, that seems to be a never-ending story, doesn't it? Looks like you disposed of some of the rats by the looks of these fresh graves, Frank. How many more you figure are left?" the marshal asked.

"A man named O'Leary is the head honcho. I don't know how many more men he has with him in Mexico, but it can't be many. And I'd like to bring him in alive if possible. It would be a great satisfaction for these people to serve him the justice he has coming," Frank said.

"I'd like to see him hang for the things he's done around here, Marshal. He's been skimming forty percent from the businesses, calling it a protection fund," the general store owner said.

"Protection fund, huh? We'll see how protected he'll be when we meet up with him," the marshal said.

"I guess we should ride out to O'Leary's ranch. I doubt he's there. I'm sure he stayed in Mexico," Frank said.

"Mexico? I'm guessing he has a place there too?" The marshal asked.

"Yes indeed, Marshal. He has quite the cattle-stealing operation going on. He would steal cattle from the area and move them to Mexico at night in a hurry," Frank said.

"This just gets more interesting by the minute. I can't wait to meet this O'Leary," the marshal replied.

Becca and Elizabeth came walking up, and Frank took his hat off as Becca walked up to him and hugged him. "Marshal, I'd like you to meet Becca," Frank said with a crooked grin.

"Well, it sure is getting more interesting by the minute. Very nice to meet you, Becca. Are you from around here?" the marshal asked.

"Yes, sir. I have a ranch outside of town a few miles," Becca replied.

"And it's a beautiful ranch, Marshal. A very heavenly setting," Frank said, blushing a little.

"I bet it is, Frank, I bet it is indeed," the marshal said with a grin. The marshal asked Elizabeth, "And who might you be, ma'am?"

"Elizabeth, sir. My husband and I live in this town. He was beaten badly by O'Leary's men, but he's gonna be all right," she replied.

"Anything you need, Marshal, just ask. I think you'll find everyone here will cooperate with you," the general store owner said.

"Thank you, sir. We're gonna bring this to an end one way or another. I promise you that," the marshal said.

"Let's go over to the saloon and get a bite to eat and have a drink. I bet you could use both after that long ride, Marshal," Frank said.

"That, my friend, is the best plan I've heard in a while," the marshal said smiling.

They went to the saloon, and Becca and Elizabeth went to the kitchen to cook up something for everyone while the men gathered at the tables and one of the men poured drinks for everyone. Frank and the marshal were sitting next to each other, and the marshal looked at Frank with a grin on his face and asked, "So tell me, Frank, you look like a changed man. Anything to do with that pretty lady back there?"

"Yes, sir. I keep pinching myself to make sure this isn't a dream or if I'm lying face-down in the desert somewhere, hallucinating from dehydration or something," Frank said.

"Well, you're not hallucinating. This is real, and we need to figure out what we're gonna do with this O'Leary and end this nightmare for these people," the marshal said.

Becca and Elizabeth brought plates of food to the men, and Frank and the marshal discussed their plans. Frank wasn't sure how many men O'Leary had with him in Mexico, but he knew they had to go there and bring him back to stand trial, and he wasn't gonna sleep until O'Leary was either O'Leary was either behind bars or dead from a rope around his neck.

They finished eating, and Frank went to the kitchen where Becca and Elizabeth were, and asked Elizabeth, "How's Tom? Is he okay?"

"Yes, he's gonna be fine, Frank," she replied.

"He's a brave man for doing what he did. Not many men would have put themselves in that kind of danger," Frank said.

"Thank you, Frank. You're a good and decent man, and thank you for pulling the men together like you have. Not many men would just show up out of the blue and help a bunch of strangers like you have," Elizabeth said.

"Well, it's all because of this pretty lady right here. She's the most amazing woman I've ever known, and I would do anything for her and anyone in her life," he said, smiling and wrapped his arms around Becca.

"Yes, she is a wonderful lady. She told me who you were, Frank, but don't worry. I won't tell anyone who you really are. I think it's great how you turned your life around, and maybe it's come full circle. Now, you can be happy and in love and make a life right here in this beautiful part of the world. Well, I better go check on Tom. I'll leave you two lovebirds alone," Elizabeth said as she walked away smiling.

"Did you mean all of that, Frank? What you said about me?" Becca asked.

"You bet I did, pretty lady. I'll do whatever it takes to keep you safe. And when this is over, you and I are gonna spend the rest of our lives laughing, loving, and bathing in that creek below your house," he said, laughing.

"That sounds great. Make sure you come back to me when you go to Mexico with the marshal. He seems like a good man. Now, I know why you turned out like you have. He's been like a father to you, hasn't he, Frank?" Becca said.

"Yes, he has been like a father to me. I owe him so much for giving me a second chance in life. I don't know how to repay him for doing that," Frank said as he put his fingertips through her hair and gently pulled her face to his and kissed those beautiful lips. "I'll be back, pretty lady. Nothing and no one is gonna come between you and me and our future together. The marshal and I have been through this before, and we'll put a stop to O'Leary. I promised to you and to the people of this town, and I'm a man of my word," Frank said sternly.

"Yes, I know you are, Frank. I sensed that about you when we had our first conversation. You're a lot like my husband in many ways but different in others," Becca said. "He would've liked you, and I know he would be okay with you and me together because he would've wanted me to move on." She kissed Frank on the cheek. "I've packed you and the marshal some sandwiches and things to take with you. I wouldn't want you to lose your energy. You're gonna need it." She then laughed.

Frank blushed a little and said, "I sure am looking forward to your to-die-for meals for the rest of my days." He smiled with that crooked grin. "Well, we better get going. It will be dark soon, and we'll use the darkness to travel. I'll see you soon, pretty lady." He kissed her one more time.

*****

The marshal and the rest of the men were outside the saloon, and Frank walked out and looked each man in the eyes and said, "Men, we know what we have to do. Up to this point, you've shown me great courage and bravery, and I won't say anything about it if you don't wanna go to Mexico. You can ride home, and nothing will be said."

The general store owner shouted back, "Frank, we wouldn't be here if it weren't for you, and we know some of us might not come back from Mexico alive. But that's a chance we're willing to take. So we're all with you, and we're all going."

Frank looked at the marshal and gave him a crooked grin and said, "This is my last one, boss. You understand why this place has my heart, don't you?"

The marshal smiled back and said, "Yes, sir. I figured I'd lose you to a beautiful woman someday, but not an entire town. I hate to lose you, my friend, but it's good to see you happy. Now, let's get moving. I wanna make it back here tomorrow to have one of those great-tasting meals Becca cooks up."

"Yes, sir. I'm looking forward to that myself," Frank said as they rode toward Old Mexico.

Chapter 11

Frank and the marshal were leading the way, and as they were heading out, Frank saw Tom looking out of the window from the doctor's office. Tom nodded his head to Frank, and Frank nodded back, as if everything would be all right.

"So how many men do you figure O'Leary has with him down there, Frank?" the marshal asked.

"Probably a dozen or so. But I'm thinking from what that little Mexican girl told us, most of them are there against their will, so I'm counting on a little help from those people," Frank replied.

"So you don't think O'Leary is very liked among the Mexicans, Frank?" the marshal responded.

"No, sir. He just has the money to buy people who need money," Frank said. "And I'm hoping when we get there, most of them won't wanna get mixed up in this."

"I hope you're right, Frank. I'd like to get this over as soon as possible and get my ass back to Santa Fe. I'm getting too old for this, and I may have to hang up my guns too, Frank. I've been doing this a long time, and this old saddle is wearing thin," the marshal said with a grin.

"Yeah, I know the feeling. I hate to give up on this line of work, but it's time for me to settle down and enjoy life before I get too old to enjoy it," Frank said. "You're welcome at the ranch anytime, Marshal, and I'd like to thank you again for giving me this opportunity as deputy marshal, I want you to know how much I appreciate it, sir."

"That's very kind of you, Frank. I knew you were a good person when I met you, and I believe in second chances. And I wish you and

Becca all the happiness life can offer you. She sure is a pretty lady, Frank," the marshal said.

"She sure is, Marshal," Frank replied.

They arrived at the tree where Becca left her wrap on a limb when Young William had her, and Frank had a warm feeling rush through him. He thought of Becca and her beauty and the majestic place she had along the foothills and wondered again if he was lying face-down in the desert, dreaming of this. He thought of Tom and Elizabeth and the little Mexican girl that young William killed. She was probably so confused and scared and wondered why all of that was happening to her. Frank knew he had to get to her parents and take them to where she was buried so they could give her a proper burial.

They arrived at the crossing and Frank turned and looked at the men and said, "This is Mexico, my friends, and there is no American law here. I can't promise you protection, so I'll say again. If any of you wanna turn around, now is the time. You, men, have proven yourselves, but this might get bloody, and some of us might not make it back alive."

"We said we are with you, Mr. Wilson, and we know the consequences. We're willing to face them. This is our lives we're dealing with and our families. You lead the way, and we'll follow," the general store owner shouted.

"All right then," Frank smiled with that crooked grin and turned to the marshal and said, "Last one, boss. Thanks again for all you've done for me."

"Same here, amigo. Let's do this and get the hell out of here," the marshal replied.

They crossed the river into Old Mexico. It was dark with a half moon, and there were a trillion stars in the sky. It was a beautiful place, and it didn't seem like there could be so much ugliness in the world. A lot of people talked of God and forgiveness and turning the other cheek, but Frank wasn't sure about all of that. He believed in a creator or creators but had seen too many bad things to believe in just a creator of goodness. There had to be a creator of evil, or we wouldn't have so much of it.

"There's a rider coming, Frank," the marshal said.

Frank saw him, and he was riding fast. Frank got off his horse and aimed his rifle toward the rider and yelled, "Stop right there! Who are you?"

"Don't shoot, amigo. Please, don't shoot," the rider shouted.

"Who are you?" Frank asked.

"I came from O'Leary's. I worked for him, me and my wife, but she died a few days ago," the rider said. He was Mexican but spoke very good English. "I don't know why she died. She went to sleep and never woke up. She was very upset that young William took our daughter, and we haven't seen her for days."

"Was your daughter about fourteen or fifteen, sir?" Frank asked.

"Si, señor. Fifteen, yes," the Mexican man replied.

"I know where your daughter is, sir. We buried her yesterday. She was killed by young William. I'm sorry, I truly am," Frank said.

The man started weeping and saying words in Spanish.

"I'll take you to her, but first, take us to O'Leary's ranch," Frank said.

"Si, señor, I'll take you there. But I must warn you, he has about twenty men with him," the Mexican man said.

"Is there any chance some of those men would turn against O'Leary?" Frank asked.

"Si. Most of us are there against our will, and if you can convince them that you are there to help us, they will turn against him," the Mexican man said.

"We want only justice to be done to O'Leary, and we aim to hang him once we get him back to the States," Frank said. "And I promise you, sir, justice will be served, so lead the way and we'll follow you." Frank added.

"Okay senor, it's only a few miles." The Mexican man said as he rode toward O'Leary's.

*****

Becca and Elizabeth were sitting at the doctor's office with Tom. He was doing better, and the doctor said he could go home tomorrow. Elizabeth looked at Becca and could see the worry on her face and said, "Don't you worry, Becca, Frank will come back to you. He knows what he's doing, and he'll be fine." She then kissed Tom on the forehead.

"Yeah. I could tell when I first met Frank that he was a man of courage and compassion. He will definitely be coming back, Becca. Don't you worry," Tom said, smiling.

"Thank you both. I feel like my heart is coming out of my chest. I'm so anxious to see him again and wrap my arms around him," Becca said anxiously. "When my husband died, I didn't know what I was gonna do about the ranch. O'Leary kept pressuring me to sell it to him, and I knew in my heart that it was the wrong thing to do. I believe Frank was sent here to help all of us, and I also believe maybe my husband had something to do with that in some way." She wept and smiled at the same time.

"It's all right, Becca. I know how you feel. I don't know if I could have been as strong as you have been if I would have lost Tom like you lost your husband," Elizabeth said.

"Your husband was a great man, and everyone like him, Becca. And I'm sure he had something to do with bringing Frank to us and you," Tom said kindly.

Becca wept a little and smiled and said, "Everything is gonna be all right. I feel it in my heart. And thank you both for lifting my spirits. I needed to hear that and say those words. I feel better now." She smiled.

Chapter 12

Frank and the men were close to O'Leary now, and Frank was thinking back on the days with Jesse and the gang. He knew in his heart back then that he was doing the right thing but not legally. He told himself that he had to do this legally with O'Leary, no matter how he felt about him, and he would like to bring him in alive if possible.

The marshal looked at Frank and asked, "Are you ready for this, Frank?"

Frank responded with confidence and said, "I've never been more ready about something in my life, Marshal."

"This is your fight, my friend. It's your call, Frank," the marshal said.

"I have a plan. It's a chance but one I feel I have to take," Frank said.

"Let's hear it, Frank," the marshal said.

Frank tipped his hat up a little and sat tall in his saddle and said, "I'm going in alone to try to have a one-on-one with O'Leary."

"You think his men will just let you ride in there and do that, Frank?" the marshal said.

"I'm betting on it. I don't think those men are there because they love O'Leary," Frank said.

"You're a crazy son of a bitch, Frank, but it's your call. We have your back," the marshal said.

Frank gave the marshal his crooked grin and wrapped a white cloth around the end of his rifle and started toward O'Leary's ranch. As he got closer, shots were fired, hitting the ground in front of him. He knew if they wanted to kill him, they could. But he felt O'Leary wanted to talk, so he pressed on toward the house. As he rode in, he counted about fifteen men and figured O'Leary had a few more inside with him.

Frank was met by three men at the front steps of the house, and one man spoke and asked, "What do you want, señor?"

"O'Leary," Frank said.

The men laughed, and the man asked Frank, "What do you want with O'Leary? I don't think he wants to talk to you, so maybe you should ride away before you get hurt, amigo."

"I can't do that, and I'm not your friend. So why don't you let me see O'Leary? You might just live to see another day," Frank boldly replied.

The three men grew restless and spoke to each other in Spanish.

Frank spoke up and said, "Just let me pass. I just want O'Leary. The rest of you are not my concern."

The man asked Frank if the little girl young William took was still alive. She was the daughter of his uncle. "I'm afraid not. Young William shot her for no reason other than he just didn't need her anymore." He then added, "He's dead. I killed him for being the cowardly son of a bitch he was."

The man looked at the other two men on the porch, and they stepped aside and said, "He's inside. He has four men with him. I can't guarantee your safety inside, but what you did to young William, I wish I could have done that to him." He looked at Frank with pride in his eyes and said, "We are poor people here. We do what we have to do to survive, even if that means we have to work for men like O'Leary."

"I understand. Now, step aside. I wanna look O'Leary in the eyes and see what kind of man he is," Frank said.

They moved out of his way, and the man yelled to the men inside to let him in. Frank could tell this man had influence on the others and hoped that influence would be in Frank's favor if the shooting was to erupt.

*****

The marshal and the other men were in disbelief that Frank was doing this, but in the years Frank and the marshal had been together, it didn't surprise the marshal. He knew Frank could take care of himself in any situation.

The general store owner was getting nervous and asked the marshal, "Do you think Mr. Wilson is going to kill O'Leary?"

The marshal grinned and said, "That depends on whether O'Leary wants to live or die."

*****

Frank walked up to the front door, and one of the men inside opened it. He heard a man with a strong Irish accent say, "You have a lot of nerve showing up here, laddy. You may not get out of here as peacefully as you came in." It was O'Leary.

"I'm giving you two options, O'Leary. Live or die?" Frank said sternly.

"Well now, those are some strong words coming from a man standing alone in my house surrounded by guns. Don't you think you should consider those options yourself?" O'Leary said, laughing.

Frank took a deep breath and snapped back at O'Leary and said, "My option is to leave here with you, dead or alive. I would rather you be alive to stand trial, and I promise you a fair trial and your safety until we return to the States."

"Fair trial? There is no such thing, and you know it, Frank. May I call you Frank? That is your name, isn't it?" O'Leary said as he walked out onto the front porch.

"Yes, that is my name. And no, you can call me Mr. Wilson, and I'm here to address the fairness situation and to see that fairness comes to everyone, including you if you choose," Frank said.

"Well, it looks like we have ourselves a crusader here, boys," O'Leary said as he laughed out loud to his men, but Frank noticed his men weren't laughing. They were looking at Frank like he was making sense, and it gave Frank the feeling that he was going to walk out of here with O'Leary alive. "You killed my boy. Why should

I do anything except shoot you down where you stand?" O'Leary shouted.

"You can try, and you might get it done. But I guarantee I will kill you and every man here before I fall, so think logically before you regret your actions. If you walk out of here with me, you will live to see another day," Frank said.

One of O'Leary's men walked up onto the porch; it was the man with influence, and he had the father of the little Mexican girl with him. The man was shaking, with tears in his eyes, as he looked at Frank and said, "Señor, you are a good man. I could tell that you were when I first met you, and I can never repay you for killing such an animal as young William. And I say to all of you, men, put down your guns. We no longer work for O'Leary. He is the devil, and with the devil comes evil. But we are not evil people. We are hungry and poor. So we will make a trade with you, Señor Wilson. We give you O'Leary, and we keep his ranch, his land, and his cattle."

"What! You are not in the position to make that deal, Francesco. This is my house and land, and I will not allow you to negotiate my property!" O'Leary shouted.

Francesco looked at O'Leary and walked over to him face-to-face and put his pistol to O'Leary's neck and said, "You're lucky I don't kill you right here, you son of a bitch. But I want you to hang for what you've done to my family and to the others."

O'Leary slowly reached for his gun, but Frank pointed his rifle at him and said, "Don't even think about it. I'll blow you out of this world."

One of the other men grabbed O'Leary's gun and threw it on the ground. Frank handed the white cloth he had tied around his rifle to Francesco and told him to tie O'Leary's hands with it as tight as he could. O'Leary had a look of fear and anger on his face as his hands were being tied by Francesco. Francesco looked at Frank and said, "You have safe passage out of Mexico, Señor Wilson, and I pray your justice system will not fail the people he has terrorized. His blood runs cold, and I hope he hangs on a hot afternoon."

"I guarantee he will hang, amigo. Good luck to you and all you men. I know it's hard, but always try to do good. Don't fall prey to evil," Frank said as he shoved O'Leary forward and started walking back to the marshal.

The men were shouting hoorahs when Frank walked O'Leary toward them and were in disbelief that he was able to pull that off. Frank stopped and looked back at Francesco to come to him. He told Francesco where his daughter was buried, and Francesco thanked him again and walked away. Frank reached the marshal, and the marshal just shook his head and grinned. Then, they headed back to New Mexico.

Chapter 13

They arrived back in town just before sunrise, and they heard some-one yell, "They made it back!"

Becca heard that and jumped up from the chair she was sleeping on inside her bedroom in the hotel and bolted out the door into the street outside and saw Frank riding in front. She looked into his eyes, and her heart melted. She was so relieved.

Frank looked at Becca and smiled like he'd never smiled before—this time, out of both sides of his mouth. Just the sight of her tamed his angry emotions and the rage in his heart for O'Leary. They reached the sheriff's office, which hadn't seen a sheriff in a long time. The last sheriff was killed by O'Leary because he wouldn't do what O'Leary asked of him.

Becca couldn't help herself; she ran to Frank and threw her arms around him and hugged him so tight his hat fell off.

"I told you I'd be back, pretty lady, and it sure feels good to be in your arms," Frank said.

"You're never leaving them again, Frank," Becca said, smiling.

The marshal cleared his throat and gave a little cough and said, "Are you gonna lock up your prisoner, Frank, or just stand there and drool all over yourself?" He then grinned.

Frank and Becca both laughed, and Frank answered, "Yes, sir. He is my prisoner, and I will be happy to lock his ass up. Excuse me, Becca, I have important matters pending."

Becca smiled and said, "Yes, you do, Frank. Very important matters." She looked him in the eyes with her beautiful big, green eyes in a flirtatious manner.

Frank turned and looked to the men and said loudly, "You, men, should be very proud of yourselves. You made a stand and believed in yourselves, and we got it done. We exterminated the rats and took back your town, and I wish all of you nothing but good health, prosperity, and love in the days ahead. I thank you for your courage. Now, go home to your families. This is your town again. Share the wealth and well-being of one another, and live peacefully with kindness and respect for your neighbors. We'll talk soon."

The general store owner spoke loudly, "We thank you, Mr. Wilson. You're a good man, and we hope you'll stay here in our town. We could use a good sheriff!" He smiled.

Frank smiled back and tipped his hat up a bit, pushed O'Leary toward the jail, walked him inside and locked the door of his cell, and said to him, "You better get used to these bars. You'll be here a while before we can get a judge here so we can give your ass a fair trial before we hang the shit out of you." Frank laughed.

The marshal was standing in the middle of the room, grinning from ear to ear, and said, "Looks like you may have found yourself a new job." He chuckled.

"Looks like it, doesn't it?" Frank said.

"Well, I guess this is it, Frank. You've finally found yourself a home and a damn good one too. It's been a pleasure, my friend. We were a good team, and I think it's about time I put these old bones to rest and retire off into the sunset. That Becca sure is a pretty woman, Frank. I think I'll get myself a room at the hotel and get a hot bath and maybe a little whiskey before heading back to Santa Fe." He grinned.

"You take care, Marshal. Thanks again for everything you've done for me. I'll never forget it," Frank said as they shook hands and parted ways.

*****

Frank walked outside. Becca and Elizabeth were talking, and Frank threw his arms around Becca and said, "How about we go get ourselves a fine dinner over at the café? Let someone else do the cooking tonight." As he smiled.

"That sounds great, Frank. Do you think O'Leary will be all right in there by himself?" she asked.

"He'll be safer in there, locked behind bars, than out here. We'll take him some food from the diner after we've eaten," Frank said. He then looked at Elizabeth and asked with that very charming crooked grin of his, "Is Tom up for a good dinner? I'm buying."

"I think he might be, Frank. I'll go get him, and we'll meet you two there," Elizabeth replied.

"Take your time. We'll get a table and order some coffee. Come on, pretty lady. It sure is a beautiful night, isn't it?" Frank said to Becca.

"Yes, it is, Frank. Yes, it is," Becca replied with a huge smile and grabbed Frank's hand, and they walked to the café.

The End

About the Author

James White grew up reading Louis L'Amour books. Westerns always fascinated him, so it was only fitting that his first novel be a Western. He spent a lot of time outdoors while growing up in Missouri. It inspired him, and he believes it made him the writer he is today.